THE
WOODLINGS
AND THE
WISH
DRAGON

Published in paperback in 2016 by the North York Moors National Park Authority

The Old Vicarage
Bondgate
Helmsley
York
YO62 5BP
www.northyorkmoors.org.uk

© North York Moors National Park Authority 2016

ISBN 978-1-904622-31-4

British Library Cataloguing in Publication Data. A catalogue record for this book is available from the British Library.

Printed in Great Britain.

THE
WOODLINGS
AND THE
WISH
DRAGON

Written by Sue Wilkinson

Illustrated by Graeme Wilkinson

Based on an idea by George Flanagan,
at The Moors National Park Centre at Danby,
who helped the Woodlings build
their amazing little houses

North York Moors National Park Education Service

Once upon a time, long ago, tiny people lived in Crow Wood. They were shy and secretive and none of the big people ever saw them. They lived in tiny houses and they were called Woodlings.

Woodruff and Willow loved to play hide and seek with the creatures in the wood.

Then one sunny day, something very strange happened.

It began to snow! Snowflakes as big as
apples floated down from the sky. The air
grew colder and colder. The streams turned
to ice. Soon everything was buried under
deep, fluffy snow.

At first Woodruff and Willow loved the snow.

They played outside until their tiny toes tingled.

Day after day, week after week, it snowed. Woodruff and Willow soon tired of being wet and cold.

The grown-up Woodlings struggled to find enough food for everyone.

The old Woodlings rubbed their bony hands together and tried to keep warm. All the Woodlings longed to see a green leaf and to feel the sun on their faces.

Then, one day there was a terrible storm.

The wind whistled.

Snowflakes swirled.

The creatures of the wood shivered in their nests and dens.

The Woodlings were huddled together in their houses when suddenly they heard a very loud…

Branches crashed to the ground.

There was a big **THUD** and the ground shook.

W oodruff crept to the window to see out. Then he
opened the door a crack and peeped through
the trees. There on the ground was a huge, crumpled
mound and…

Woodruff tiptoed towards the creature. He could feel its hot breath blowing out of two huge nostrils that were as big as rabbit holes.

Its eyes were shut tight like cracks in rock.

"It must have crashed in the storm," said Woodruff. "I think it's hurt."

The other Woodlings crowded round to see.

Then, Mugwort, the oldest and wisest Woodling, pushed to the front.

"It's a Wish Dragon!" he said in amazement.

"We have to help it."

So the Woodlings set to work.
Woodruff untangled the dragon's crumpled wings and cleaned its wounds with soft snow.

Willow polished the scales on the dragon's back until they gleamed like gold coins.

The Woodlings worked all through the day and all through the night until they were cold and hungry but…

The dragon lay still, it didn't stir.
Not a sniff, not a snore, not a peep, not a purr.
From the tip of its tail to the top of its head,
The dragon lay still… perhaps it was dead?

The next day and the next day, the Woodlings looked after the dragon but...

The dragon lay still, it didn't stir.
Not a sniff, not a snore, not a peep, not a purr.
From the tip of its tail to the top of its head,
The dragon lay still... perhaps it was dead?

The next day Woodruff and Willow were sweeping snow off the dragon's back when suddenly...

A huge eye opened!
A moment later the other eye
opened and then without warning…

The dragon sneezed.

The Woodlings tumbled to the ground and Woodruff was sprayed with dragon snot that stuck to him like cake icing.

The dragon shook and stretched out its wings.

"Woodlings," said the dragon in a deep voice that rumbled like thunder.

"The kindness you've given, I will repay,
I will protect you, for ever and a day.
In times of trouble, over sea or land,
Your greatest wish is my command."

Mugwort stepped forward.

"Wish Dragon," he said. "We are in great trouble now. This winter is never-ending. The woodland and all its creatures are cold and hungry.

We wish that this winter would end and that we could see a green leaf and feel the sun on our faces."

The Wish Dragon nodded, took a deep breath and turned to the frozen river. Then from its mouth came a whoosh of red hot flames and sparks. The frozen river began to melt, until it was once again splashing over mossy, green rocks.

The dragon blew its fiery breath again and again. The snow began to melt. The clouds parted and sunlight shone down and warmed the faces of the Woodlings.

The Woodlings cheered and clapped and danced, and thanked the dragon a hundred times.

Woodruff and Willow kicked off their boots and jumped into the stream to splash and play.

The grown-up Woodlings set about collecting food to prepare a feast.

The old Woodlings held their wrinkled faces up to the warm sunshine and smiled. The never-ending winter had ended at last.

The Wish Dragon found a comfy spot by the river and lay down to sleep. There it stayed for the rest of its days, keeping watch over the Woodlings, ready to grant their wishes in times of trouble.

Some of the Woodlings named their houses in honour of the Wish Dragon and his fiery breath.

Some of these names, such as Furnace Farm and Fryup Dale, are still in use today. A search on the map will confirm the truth of this tale.

Did you know...

The Woodling houses really do exist. They can be found within the grounds of The Moors National Park Centre at Danby in the North York Moors National Park.

Why don't you visit this lovely place and see for yourself?

What is a National Park?

Almost every country in the world has treasured areas called National Parks. These areas are carefully looked after to ensure that everyone will be able to enjoy their special qualities in the future. Find out more about the North York Moors National Park at www.northyorkmoors.org.uk